Prince Bear

Prince Bear

Translated from the German

Helme Heine

Margaret K. McElderry Books
NEW YORK

Prince Bear

Long, long ago—when fairy tales were young—every bear could change into a prince, and every princess could change into a bear.

If a bear grew tired of living in the forest, fishing,
and hunting, he waited at the roadside until
a princess drove by.

Then he greeted her, climbed into her fine carriage, and kissed her. He turned into a prince at once. Together, they rode on to the castle, where he lived very happily and well.

If a princess felt bored with living in a castle and always being sweet and good, she jumped onto her horse and galloped into the forest.

There, she kissed the first bear she met,

changed into a bear, and quickly climbed a tree.

Or she stole some honey.

Or she swam and fished.

Life was simple. Everyone was happy and contented.

Then one day, a woodcutter came into the forest and began to cut down all the trees that the bears loved to climb.

Roads were built, which were very dangerous   to cross.

Now the bears had to get licenses to hunt and fish.
They were no longer happy to be bears. Instead,
they all wanted to be princes or princesses.

If a princess bicycled into the forest to look for
mushrooms, the bears all chased her, asking
for a kiss.

At last, no princess was allowed to leave the castle
alone. And no princess wanted to be a bear anymore.

Finally, the bears marched up to the castle.
They growled loudly and demanded to be let in,
so they could kiss the princesses.

But the princesses threw things and shouted
at them to go away. There were too many in the
castle already because none of the princesses
wanted to be turned into bears any longer.

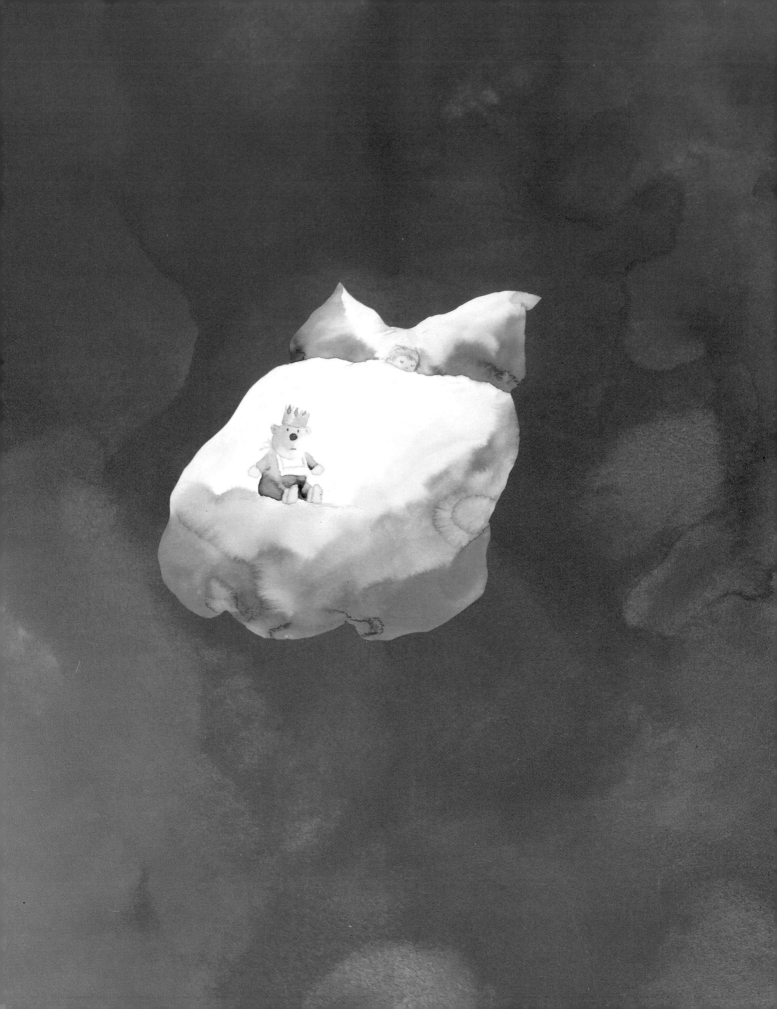

Ever since then, no bear can turn into a
prince, and no princess can change into
a bear, no matter how often they kiss.

Originally published under the title *Prinz Bär* by Gertraud Middelhauve Verlag, Köln
Copyright © 1987 by Gertraud Middelhauve Verlag GmbH & Co. KG, Köln
English translation copyright © 1989 by Margaret K. McElderry Books,
a division of Macmillan Publishing Company

Margaret K. McElderry Books
Macmillan Publishing Company
866 Third Avenue,
New York, NY 10022
Collier Macmillan Canada, Inc.

Printed in U.S.A.
First American Edition

10 9 8 7 6 5 4 3 2 1

Library of Congress Cataloging-in-Publication Data

Heine, Helme.
Prince Bear.
Translation of: Prinz Bär.
Summary: Recounts how in the olden days any bear
in the forest could change into a prince and any
princess could change into a bear, and how this
happy balance was upset so bears and princesses
eventually could no longer trade places.
[1. Bears—Fiction.   2. Fairy tales]   I. Title.
PZ8.H364Pr   1989   [E]   88-32576
ISBN 0-689-50484-5